KT-484-388

Bear and Bird

The PICNIC and other stories

JARVIS

WALKER BOOKS

For Jenna

This is a work of fiction. Names, characters, places and incidents are either the product of the author's imagination or, if real, used fictitiously. All statements, activities, stunts, descriptions, information and material of any other kind contained herein are included for entertainment purposes only and should not be relied on for accuracy or replicated as they may result in injury.

First published 2023 by Walker Books Ltd
87 Vauxhall Walk, London SE11 5HJ

2 4 6 8 10 9 7 5 3 1

Text and illustrations © 2023 Jarvis

The right of Jarvis to be identified as author of this work has been asserted in accordance with the Copyright, Designs and Patents Act 1988

This book has been typeset in Adobe Garamond Pro

Printed and bound in China

All rights reserved. No part of this book may be reproduced, transmitted or stored in an information retrieval system in any form or by any means, graphic, electronic or mechanical, including photocopying, taping and recording, without prior written permission from the publisher.

British Library Cataloguing in Publication Data:
a catalogue record for this book is available from the British Library

ISBN 978-1-5295-0489-7

www.walker.co.uk

CONTENTS

The Flower

BING-BONG!

Bear and Bird had a big day planned.

Bird was early.

"I'll be out in a minute," shouted Bear from his big bed. "I haven't just woken up. I promise!"

Bird waited outside on the large comfy petals of a new flower and wondered what kind of day they would have.

Then she fell in.

Bird was *inside* a flower and could not get out.

"Sorry I'm late!" said Bear. "I thought my feet would move quicker than they did."

Bear looked around. "Bird? That's odd. Are you there?"

Bear heard something.

It sounded like *crying*. But where?

He couldn't see anyone.

Bear decided to ignore his eyes and follow his ears.

Surely not, thought Bear.

It can't be. It is.

It's a flower.

And it's very upset.

How can I cheer up a flower?

Hmm. If only Bird were here.

She'd know what to do.

Bear scratched his head until he had an idea.

“Hello, Flower!” said Bear.

“I know how to cheer you up. Let me tell you all about my friend Bird.

"Bird is SO silly that she once thought that the moon had fallen into the water. *Tee-hee!*

"Bird is SO silly that she once tried to stick all the leaves back on the trees, because she thought they were broken. *Tee-hee!*

"Bird is SO silly that—"

"Shush!" said the flower.

"Well, aren't you rude!" said Bear. "I was only trying to cheer you up. In that case, I'm going to find my very best friend, Bird. She wouldn't talk to me like that. Silly flower!"

And Bear stomped away.

"Don't go! Come back! Help me!" yelled the flower.

Bear felt bad.

How do I help a flower? he wondered. Then he remembered that flowers need water.

Bear filled up a bucket and came back.

SPLOOOSSSH!

“There we are. Did that help at all?” said Bear.

“No!” said the flower. “Help! I’m stuck!”

"Stuck?" said Bear. "Aren't all flowers stuck? I've certainly never seen any walking around."

"I'm *not* a flower," said the flower.

This made Bear laugh.

"Well, you *look* like a flower."

Bear put his nose right up to the petals and took a big sniff.

"And you *smell* like a flower."

Bear's nose was now very tickly and twitchy and he couldn't help but—

Bear sneezed, and some of the flower's petals blew off and into the wind.

Bird tumbled out.

"Bird!" said Bear. "There you are. Oh, have I got something to show you! Look – a *talking* flower.

"Flower, say hello to my friend Bird – the one I was telling you about."

The flower didn't say anything. Because, after all, it *was* a flower.

"Oh," said Bear. "It was talking a minute ago. It really was."

Bird looked at Bear and shook her head.

"A talking flower? Bear, you are SO silly."

The Picnic

Bear and Bird were finally off on their picnic.

"Have you been to the toilet?" said Bird.

"Yes," said Bear.

Bear had *not* been to the toilet.

"Did you pack the music player?" said Bird.

"Yes," said Bear.

Bear had *not* packed the music player.

"And the deckchairs?" said Bird.

"Yes," said Bear.

No deckchairs, either.

"And most importantly – have you packed the picnic?" said Bird.

There was a bit of a pause before Bear said, "Yes. I've packed the picnic."

Bear had *not* packed the picnic.

"Great," said Bird.
"What a wonderful picnic
we're going to have."
"Yes," said Bear.

Bird would not be *at all* happy
if she knew that Bear had forgotten
all of the picnic things.

So, instead, it was better to say
that he had them.

That way, Bird would be happy.

Bear preferred to make Bird happy.

“Shall we put the music player on while we walk?” said Bird.

“Yes,” said Bear. “We *could* do that. But…”

“But?” said Bird

“But why don’t we sing a song instead? Let’s sing ‘The Wobble Song’,” said Bear.

Bird loved “The Wobble Song”.

And so they sang “The Wobble Song” and Bird was very happy.

The Wobble Song

You've gotta wobble wobble wobble,
Like a bubble bubble bubble.
If you wiggle wiggle wiggle,
There'll be trouble trouble trouble.

"Time for a rest," said Bird. "Where shall we put the deckchairs?"

"Deckchairs?" said Bear. "We *could* sit on the deckchairs, of course. But…"

"But?" said Bird.

"But there is a *swing* over on that tree. Let's sit on that instead," said Bear.

Bird looked at Bear.

Then she looked at Bear's rucksack.

Then the swing.

"Good idea!" said Bird. "What a great day it has been … *so far*."

Bear knew that it was nearly time for the picnic. The picnic that he *hadn't* packed.

"Right, then," said Bird. *"Picnic time."*

Bear pretended he hadn't heard.

"Picnic time!" said Bird, a little louder.

"Yes. The picnic. Yes," said Bear. "We *could* eat the picnic that I have most definitely packed. But..."

"But?" said Bird.

There was a long pause.

"But I think you once said ... *nature is to be nibbled*."

"I did?" said Bird.

"Yes. You are very wise. So, here, taste *this*."

Bear handed Bird a leaf.

Bird looked at Bear.

Then she looked at the rucksack.

Then the leaf.

Bird took a bite and began to chew.

Everything was resting on this leaf. This randomly plucked leaf. This slightly soggy leaf.

Bird stopped chewing.

Then she chewed a bit more.

"Bear," said Bird.

"Yes?" said Bear.

“It’s … *delicious*,” said Bird.

Bear could breathe again.

“Yes,” said Bear. “I know.”

Bear and Bird spent the afternoon eating leaves.

“I’ve had a really *wonderful* day,” said Bird. “But…”

“But?” said Bear, clutching the empty rucksack.

"But it's time to go back now," said Bird.

Bear would not be at all happy if he knew that Bird *knew* that he had forgotten all of the picnic things.

So, instead, it was better to say nothing. That way, Bear would be happy. Bird preferred to make Bear happy.

And so they both went back to Bird's house and Bear headed straight for the toilet. He was absolutely bursting.

The Painting

“What a perfect afternoon for painting,” said Bird, setting up the easels and brushes in her garden.

“I’ve only ever painted once,” said Bear. “And that was my front door. So I don’t think I’ll be any good.”

“It doesn’t matter, Bear. Anyone can paint,” said Bird. “Hey, let’s paint that tree.”

Bird knew all about being a painter.

She shared some advice like: “Close one eye” and “Stand back from your painting, scratch your chin and say ‘Hmm’”.

"How's it going, Bird?" asked Bear.

"Really great. I *love* painting. Painting is *so* much fun. How about you?" asked Bird.

"OK," said Bear.

"Can I see?" asked Bird.

"Yes, but it's not finished yet," said Bear.

Bird had a peek.

It was unbelievable.

It was beautiful.

It was even better than the real-life tree.

"What do you think?" asked Bear.

Bird looked at Bear's painting and then looked at her own.

She shrugged.

"It's a fine start – for a beginner," said Bird.

Bird sat down and tried to make hers look better. Frantically. She was really concentrating now. But it just kept getting worse and worse.

“Wowee!” said Rabbit. “Bear’s painting is *amazing*. Squirrel! Badger! Come and look at what Bear has made.”

Pretty soon there was a large crowd gathered behind Bear, clapping and cheering at every brushstroke.

Then they looked at Bird's picture. There was no clapping or cheering. No anything.

Bird sank into her seat. Painting wasn't fun any more.

"What are *you* painting, Bird?" asked Squirrel, trying not to laugh.

And with that, Bird lobbed the painting up in the air and marched into the woods in a huff.

"'Oh, *Bear*, you're so *wonderful*. *Bear*, you're a *genius*. *Bear*, you're the *best*! Oh, and by the way, *Bird* – you're *terrible*!'

"I HATE painting," said Bird.

Bear came looking for Bird.

"Ah, there you are," said Bear.

Bird didn't say anything.

She didn't feel like talking.

Bear shuffled up next to her.

"Bird. Your painting," said Bear. "Can I have it? It would look perfect in my reading room."

"My painting?" said Bird. "Mine? You like it?"

"Oh, it's wonderful," said Bear. "It's very – interesting."

"It's upside down," said Bird.

"It's *so* good, it looks great any way up," said Bear.

Bear didn't really like the painting.
I mean, look at it.

But he liked Bird a lot, and it would remind him of her and so, in a way, it *was* a beautiful painting.

Bear said he would take it home, and as he was leaving, Bird shouted, "I'll make you lots more paintings, Bear! One for every corner of your house!"

Lucky Bear.

The Blanket

Bear was at home, snuggly and warm, under his blanket.

"This blanket is so warm and fluffy," said Bear. "It's absolutely perfect. I do *not* want to move. *Nothing* will make me move. Literally nothi—"

BING-BONG!

"Hi, Bear," said Bird. "Are you coming out to watch the sunset?"

"Umm. I would..." said Bear. "But I'm actually *really* busy. Something quite important has come up. Something that needs my attention."

Bird thought this was very odd. Bear loved to watch the sunset.

"I guess I'll go and watch the sunset on my own," said Bird.

Bear shut the door and jumped back under the blanket.

"Oh, yes. That's the good stuff," said Bear. "It's fluffy-fluffy time. I am *so* relaxed. I can't think of anything better than—"

BING-BONG!

"Hi, Bear," said Bird. "For some reason, watching the sunset wasn't very fun on my own. I wondered if you wanted to go and get some apple crumble from Badger's stall?"

Bear's belly was very grumbly and rumbly.

"You know what?" said Bear. "I'm not hungry."

Grumbly rumbly...

"You *sound* hungry," said Bird.

"No, no," said Bear.

Grumbly rumbly...

"Not me."

Grumbly rumbly...

“That sound is thunder, I think. Probably a storm.”

“OK,” said Bird, looking up at the clear night sky.

Bird thought this was all very odd.

Bear *never* said no to crumble. Sometimes he would even have *two*.

Perhaps he was sick.

She decided to bring him back some minty tea. That always made *her* feel better.

Bear shut the door and out came the blanket.

"Oh, what a blanket you are," said Bear. "I just want to hug you and smoosh you and I'm going to call you Suzie. My smooshy, soft Suzie Woozie."

Bird came back from Badger's with the minty tea.

She was just about to ring the *BING-BONG* when she overheard Bear talking. *Suzie Woozie? Who's Suzie Woozie?* thought Bird.

Bird's beak went all sniffy.

Bird's eyes went all blinky.

She felt a lot like crying.

Instead, she took a big breath and—

BING-BONG!

"So you've got a new friend called Suzie Woozie," said Bird. "And you don't want to be with me and I don't know why and I don't like watching the sunset on my own or eating crumble on my own and I thought we were best friends and now I'm sad and I brought you some minty tea and, well, what do you say about all that?"

"Oh, Bird, I am sorry," said Bear. "You *are* my best friend. Please don't be upset with me. I know just how to make you feel better. Come inside."

Bear whipped out the blanket and tucked Bird in tight.

"Ooh. This is unbelievable," said Bird. "So warm and soft. Bear, I think there's probably room for two?"

And so Bear and Bird snuggled up in the blanket called Suzie. They laughed about the talking flower, and the picnic that never was, and Bird's beautiful painting.

"Oh, Bird," said Bear. "I don't ever want to ever get out from underneath this—"

BING-BONG!

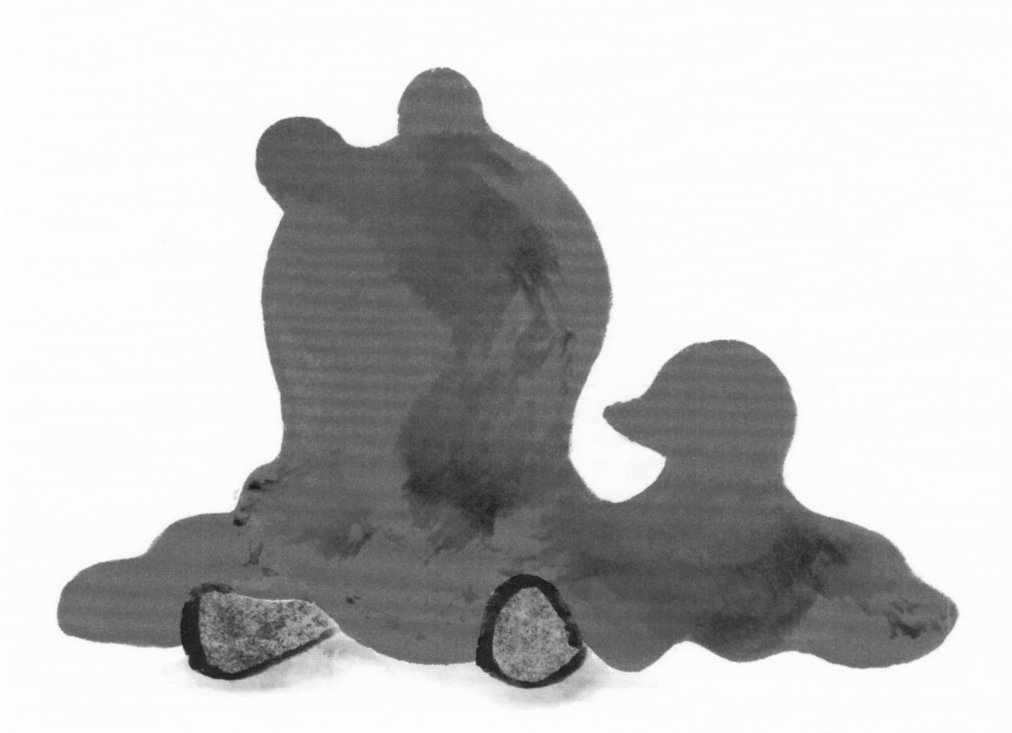

"Hello, Bear and Bird. Fancy a game of Moonbugs?" said Pig.

"Oh. Thank you. But we're busy, I'm afraid," said Bear.

"Yes," said Bird. "Something's come up. Something important. *Urgent*, in fact. Maybe tomorrow."

It was blanket time.